JOSH Gets a Bird

Written by
Joseph Wiseman &
Heather Wiseman

Illustrated by Catherine Rogotova

CHAPTERS

CHALLENGE WORDS

Door

Doorbell

High/higher

Parakeet

Whistle

Wondered

CHAPTER 1

Flying with Birds

It was a warm day at the end of summer, and Josh was swinging in his backyard.

Josh liked to watch the birds sitting in his tree and flying over his house.

He liked to see the little
birds hop around his yard
looking for bugs.

He wondered what it would be like to fly like a bird.

"Maybe if I swing higher, I can fly too!" said Josh.

So he pumped his legs
front and back as hard as
he could. Soon he was
swinging up high with the
birds!

Josh wondered what it would be like to have a pet bird, so he went to find his mom.

She was feeding Eva mashed peas.

"May I have a pet bird?" Josh asked.

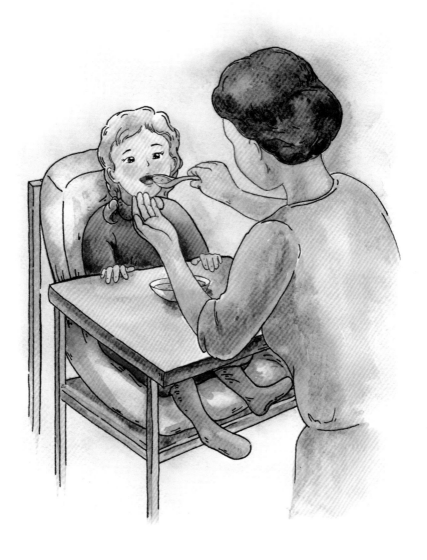

Mom smiled and then said, "Yes, but first you must learn how to care for a bird and choose what kind of bird is best for you."

"How do I choose which
bird to get?" asked Josh.

"We have some books about birds on the bookshelf," said Mom.

Mom helped Josh look for a book about all the kinds of birds.

"Now you can look for
the kind of bird that is
best for you," said Mom.

Josh looked and looked
at all the birds in the book.

The macaws were
very pretty with so many
colors, but Mom
said no.

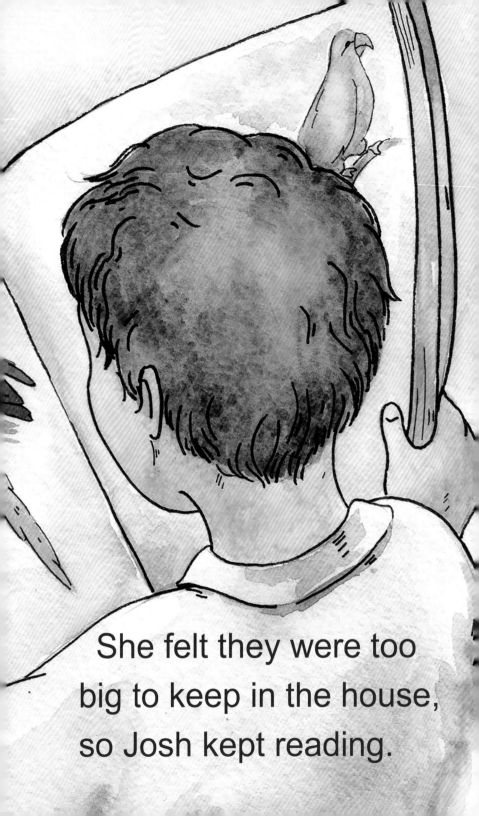

She felt they were too
big to keep in the house,
so Josh kept reading.

"This falcon looks fun. Maybe he would hunt for me," said Josh.

Mom said that falcons were not good pets for little boys.

Josh kept reading.

"Look at this bird, Mom!" He jumped up and showed her the book as she was rocking Eva to sleep.

"I saw one of these at a bird show

last year. It's called a
kook-a-bur-ra."

Josh read each part of
the name very slowly.

"It sang such pretty songs! May I have a kookaburra bird?" Josh begged Mom.

Mom said with a sad look, "No, they live in Australia. We can't buy one here where we live."

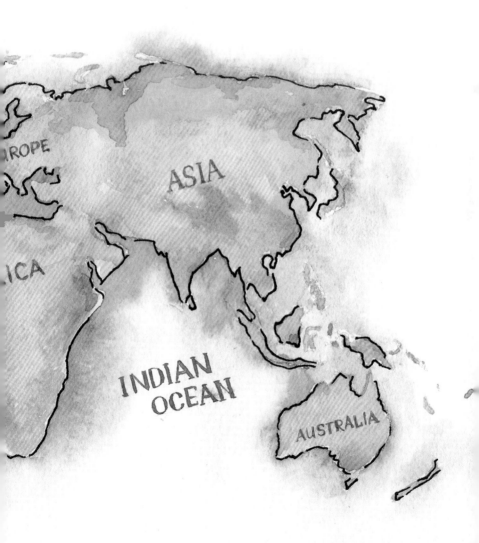

"What kind of bird can I
have then?" asked Josh.
"I need one that doesn't
cost too much, but can
still whistle."

"A finch costs the least, but it won't whistle," Mom said.

Josh did not want a finch. He looked in his book again and read some more.

"Can I get a parakeet? They can whistle!" Josh said, hoping Mom would say yes this time.

"Yes, I think a parakeet is just what you need," said Mom happily.

CHAPTER 2
Working with Mom

As soon as Eva fell asleep, Josh asked, "Can I go get my parakeet now?"

"No, now you need to earn the money to buy the parakeet," said Mom.

"You can start by helping me make some bread, and I will give you a dollar."

Josh asked Mom, "How much does a parakeet cost?"

"A pet parakeet will cost fifteen dollars," said Mom.

"Oh, that is a lot of money." Josh's face fell.

"How can I make that much money?" Josh asked with a frown.

"Just keep helping Dad and me with jobs. Save your money, and soon you will have what you need," Mom said with a smile.

"Now let's make the bread," she said to Josh.

"How do you make bread?" asked Josh.

"We need to get out the flour, water, yeast, salt, and butter," said Mom.

Josh got the flour, water, and butter.

He mixed everything and put it in a pan to rise.

"You can take out the trash while it rises," said Mom.

Josh went around the house. He picked up the trash and took it to the trash bin that was kept in the side yard by the tall bush.

"Josh, the bread is done rising. Now it's time to bake it!" called Mom.

Josh ran back to the kitchen to help Mom.

"Now we will put it in the oven, and you can set the timer," Mom said as she showed him the buttons.

"It will tell you when the bread is done."

Josh liked baking. It was so much fun!

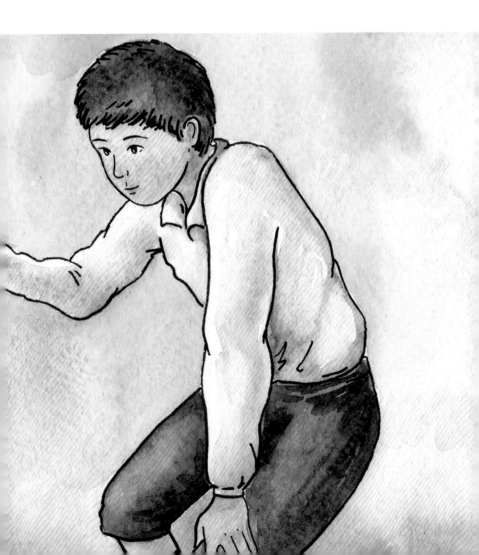

Josh went to read more about parakeets.

He read about the cages they need and the food they eat.

"Ding!" went the oven timer in the kitchen.

Mom called Josh in to help her with the bread.

"Good baking, Josh!" Mom said as she set the fresh, hot bread pans on the counter.

"You have three pans of bread, but we only need two. Who can you give this last one to?"

Josh had an idea. "Do you think that Mrs. Rose likes bread?" he asked.

Mrs. Rose was
a kind widow
who lived across
the street and
had pretty
flowers in her
front yard.

"Yes, she would love to have your extra bread," said Mom.

"Can you take this one to her house?"

Josh was happy to help. He took the bread to Mrs. Rose, who was outside watering her flowers. She looked over at him.

"Hello, Mrs. Rose! I have some bread for you!" Josh smiled at her.

"I'm helping my mom today so I can earn money to buy a parakeet."

"Thank you for the bread, Josh. This smells so good!" Mrs. Rose said.

Josh went home, and Mom gave him a big hug.

"Thank you for helping today. You earned a dollar. You have just fourteen more to go!" said Mom as she gave Josh the dollar.

CHAPTER 3

Working with Dad

The next day Josh woke up with big plans to earn more money. "I'm going to help Dad outside."

Josh found Dad pulling weeds in the garden.

"Can I help you?" asked Josh. "I'm trying to earn money to buy a parakeet."

"Yes, you can help me pull weeds from the garden. I will give you three dollars if you can weed all three rows," said Dad.

"Josh, did you know that
when I was little I had a
parakeet?" Dad asked.

"I didn't know that," Josh
said as he looked at Dad
with a big smile.

"I was about your age," Dad said. "His name was Beaker, and he was green.

He was a happy bird. He was my first pet, and he could say his name."

Dad talked like a bird and said, "Beaker!" Josh giggled.

"He does sound funny! I hope my parakeet can talk too," Josh said to Dad.

"Why do we need to pull the weeds?" asked Josh.

"So that our plants will grow bigger and stronger," said Dad as he worked.

"The weeds will block out the sun and take all the water from the plants if we don't pull them."

"Then let's pull out all the weeds!" said Josh.

"Josh, you can pick the weeds by the carrots," said Dad as he looked at Josh.

"Just try not to pull out any carrots," he said.

Josh looked at his hand. "I think I pulled out a carrot!" he said.

"It's fine. You can eat that one," said Dad. "But now that you see what they look like, you won't pull any more, will you?"

"I won't," Josh said as he looked at the carrot. It was ripe and ready to eat.

Then Josh had another idea. "Dad, may I sell some of the carrots and peas to help earn money for my parakeet?"

"That is a great idea, Josh!" Dad said. "Let's finish pulling the weeds; then you can harvest some carrots and peas to sell."

Josh kept working until his row was all finished.

"There are no more weeds by the carrots, Dad," said Josh.

"Great! There are no more weeds by the peas! Let's get some peas and carrots for you to sell," Dad said to Josh with a big smile.

Dad gave Josh three
dollars for his work pulling
the weeds.

CHAPTER 4

Peas and Carrots

Josh put some carrots
and peas into his shiny
green cart.

"Dad, will you come with me?" asked Josh.

"Yes, let's go to Mr. Jones' house first," said Dad.

They walked to Mr. Jones' house and saw him mowing his lawn.

"Hello, Mr. Jones," said Josh with a big grin.

"Hello! What are you doing with all those veggies?" asked Mr. Jones as he waved.

"I am selling veggies to earn money to buy a parakeet," said Josh, holding up a carrot.

"May I have some?" asked Mr. Jones. "I will give you two dollars."

Mr. Jones picked out the veggies he wanted.

"Here are two dollars."
Mr. Jones gave Josh the
dollar bills.

"Thank you for your
help!" said Josh.

"Let's go to Mrs. Richards' house now," said Dad. Josh sold veggies to Mrs. Richards. She paid him three dollars.

He sold some to the Smith family and some more to Mrs. Cox. Soon he had earned fifteen dollars. He was so happy!

On the way home, Josh
was tired from pulling his
cart. Just then he saw
Mrs. Rose picking apples
from her tree.

She looked very tired
too. Josh wanted to go
home and rest, but Dad
said, "Let's stop and help
her pick apples."

So Josh stopped at Mrs.
Rose's yard. "May we
help you?" asked Josh.

"Yes, I would love some help!" said Mrs. Rose.

"You can put the apples in this bag." Mrs. Rose gave Josh a big bag.

While Dad picked and
Josh bagged the apples,
Mrs. Rose talked to them.

"How much money have you earned for your parakeet?" she asked.

"I have fifteen dollars now, so I can buy my bird," said Josh.

"Where will you keep your parakeet when you get him?" asked Mrs. Rose.

"I want his cage to be in my room," said Josh.

Josh stopped working. "Oh no! I didn't ask how much money a bird cage would cost."

Josh was sad. He wouldn't be able to get his bird yet. He needed to buy a cage too and could not pay for one yet.

"Oh dear. Thank you for helping me," said Mrs. Rose, looking at Josh. "I hope you get your parakeet soon."

"Goodbye," called Josh. He and Dad were very tired as they walked home pulling the empty cart.

CHAPTER 5

Josh Gets a Surprise

When Josh got home, he showed his mom all the money he had made that day.

"That's a lot of money. Do you have what you need to buy your bird?" Mom asked.

"Yes," he said. "But I can't get it yet. I still need to earn more money to buy a cage."

"I forgot that you will need a cage. Don't be sad—you can do more work tomorrow," said Mom as she gave Josh a hug.

Then they heard the
doorbell ring. Josh ran to
open the door.

Mrs. Rose was standing there with a big grin. She was hiding something behind her back.

"I was so glad that you helped me today. I wanted to do something nice for you," she said.

"Then I remembered that this bird cage and bird seed

have been in my attic. I do not need them anymore. Would you like to have them for your parakeet?"

Josh hugged Mrs. Rose and said, "Yes! I would love to have them, please!"

"Let's go to the pet store," said Mom.

The family drove to the pet store.

At the pet store, there were green, blue, and yellow parakeets.

"There are so many parakeets. I can't choose one," said Josh.

"I like the green one," said Mom.

"I like the blue one," said Dad.

"Yellow!" said baby Eva.

"I think I want to get that one!" said Josh as he saw the one that he liked best.

It had a yellow head with red cheeks and a green body. It hopped around the cage singing.

"That one looks so happy," said Josh as the parakeet hopped a bit more and chirped.

Josh paid the clerk, and
they took the bird home.

He put it in the cage
from Mrs. Rose and gave

it food and water.

Soon the happy bird was
chirping and singing.

"What are you going to name the bird?" Dad asked Josh.

"It's a big surprise. I will tell you soon," said Josh with a small smile.

Then Mrs. Rose came over to see Josh's new parakeet.

"Thank you for the cage," said Josh. "Now I have a surprise for you."

"What is it?" she asked as she looked at him.

"I am going to name my parakeet Rosy!" Josh said and smiled at Mrs. Rose. She smiled back at him.

He was glad that he got a
pet parakeet, but he was
even more glad that he
had helped Mrs. Rose.